INTERCONNECTED

ISBN Hardcover: 979-8-9997733-7-1

ISBN Paperback: 979-8-9997733-4-0

ISBN Ebook: 979-8-9997733-6-4

Cover design: Daniel de Llano
Interior design: Megan Sheer

This book contains references to:

– Sexual content and explicit language

– Chemsex, drug use and addictive behaviors

– Mentions of extreme sexual practices

– Mental health struggles: shame, isolation and emotional shutdown

– Body image issues and social pressure

– References to overdose and other risky behaviors

INTERCONNECTED

SEX
DOPAMINE
AND Us

AN EXPERIMENTAL, GAY, SHORT NON-FICTION BOOK

Daniel de Llano

"FOREWORDS"

[*That* moment — quiet, almost invisible]

- [Daniel] *When?*
  When did I lose myself,
  and start looking for myself
  inside other people's bodies?

- [Daniel] *Maybe the day survival got*
  mixed up with speed,
  desire with dopamine,
  freedom with repetition.
  Somewhere in that intersection
  between noise and truth,
  loud parties and that strange,
  private silence afterward.
  That moment.
  When joy becomes noise,
  when noise becomes habit,

and when habit starts screaming
louder than ourselves.

- **[Daniel]** *I couldn't stop.*

- **[Daniel]** *Life did it for us.*

- **[Daniel]** *I just wanted connection…*
  the one after the noise fades.

- **[Daniel]** *Now, we're here,*
  just trying to stay happy.
  We still have "our days."

- **[Daniel]** *We still have "our days."*

A DIFFICULT CHIT-CHAT:

Disclaimer 1: This book can be triggering AF. We will be talking and thinking about sex, drugs, addictions, depression, sadness, emptiness, and many other bad things.

More important, it is going to lead you to a conversation that maybe you're not ready to have.

If you end up shaken like a maraca, I'm telling you in advance: Close this book. It could make you think, and sometimes that can be scarier than a horror movie.

Although… it could also help you re-direct the sense of who you truly are for the better.

Disclaimer 2: The characters, events, and anecdotes presented in this book are fictionalized composites based on the author's observations and research. Any resemblance to actual persons, living or dead, is entirely coincidental.

AGREEMENTS: READER-AUTHOR

I have a theory that we are all interconnected by the people we fucked with. I have fucked with someone who fucked someone who fucked someone who is friends with…

Someone who fucked with someone who fucked with you and all that, and vice versa!

So, we are closer friends than we might think! Isn't it amazing?!

As we are so close now, and before you move on, I need your EXPLICIT permission to call you:

Sweetie

Sweetie pie and derivates

My love

Baby

Bitch

...

Yes/No..........

Why? Because I'm not here as the coach, as the hypnotherapist, as the "boring, old, and stiff" person I might seem to be sometimes. I'm here to talk to YOU, as a friend who, in his own way, has been in the same sex loop you know. Apps, instant sex, sex clubs, sex-besties "you can count on" [for the record, my last sex-besties are in Spain. Not in San Francisco], etc. I need to be very direct and very myself to put on paper something so tricky. Can I count on your openness?

Like you, I have had different stages in my life. Until, one day I saw something was becoming stronger than my own decisions… It didn't end up very well…

That led me to conversations with other queer friends, and that, led me here.

So bitch, let's hold hands and walk through a difficult topic together.

Together, we got this because we are:

Interconnected.

FINAL AGREEMENT

We have been talking about how WE are going to talk to each other. It's time to talk about a different kind of conversation/agreement.

Simple. Are you brave enough to look at your own shit with realness?

Consider this a reader-to-innerself agreement:

Yes/No..........

I'm being very Spaniard with these agreements. Thank you for allowing me this space to be myself.

If both agreements says Yes: Vamos, darling. Prepare a cocktail [Mine is ready].

CHARACTERS

Me - Myself (My credentials are at the end of the book if you need them, but like you, I'm more than professional labels)

You - A radiant soul

Many People - It could be us. But as we are healthy, aligned, and we work on ourselves, it's not. Right?

Jason - He could be Daniel or Peter but he's Jason. A Stage 3 mind… You'll understand it later.

Sweetie - A cute guy. It could be you. But he's Sweetie.

THE SCENE

In a world of AK47 dicks, hungry holes, and sniffy noses… a lost Spaniard decided to talk about genuine connections. And I'm not talking about real love, soul mates, and sticky partners. I'm talking about what being truly connected means FOR US. And here is where the problem lies.

Who is really choosing?

Is it really you?

Or is it a version of you created over time that you can't escape from?

We see ourselves often, scrolling on apps and sometimes *"some kind of need"* takes us to the point of doing it in front of our family, our friends, and our partner, causing our loved ones to wonder if they are enough for us.

Yes, sweetie. Sometimes, we don't even realize we're doing it. The weird "need to hunt" is stronger than our social shame. Around us, people can feel that whatever is in our phone is more important than a real life connection, and I know that *the real us* doesn't like that.

But, what is that *some kind of need* I mentioned before?

It's the need to feel connected, but somehow getting out of control.

There. I said it. Let me break it down for you.

As humans, we are wired to stay connected. It used to mean shelter, protection, food… Being rejected meant dying. I'm not being dramatic, sweetie. If our tribe kicked us out, we would have to cross the jungle. I don't know about you, but I'd die before even seeing the first puma. Quickly. So we need to avoid abandonment and rejection at all costs. This is how we are naturally wired.

Unfortunately, we grow up in a world that creates in many of us wounds of abandonment and rejection… until one day… we come out of the closet. Suddenly questions like *what does it mean to be gay?* start popping up in our heads. And there we go. To the apps. To connect. First rubbing the eggplant and maybe later we can have a talk, right?

Early on, we get hooked on the *easy to connect catalog, because it's not gonna happen in the supermarket* lifestyle, and we get in the trap of connecting, trashing,

connecting, trashing, maybe repeating, trashing...
Let's keep it superficial, because why have one if we
can have a bunch, right?

On the other hand, after years of navigating the
closeted world, when we are finally free, we need
validation. It feels good. It reassures us.

Straight culture gives people a clear script:

fuck → **date** → **settle** → **family** → **sense of purpose
accomplished!**

In queer culture, we're still inventing our script... The
sources of "purpose" are different and we try to find
them while carrying the wounds of rejection. In the
meantime, let's just fuck! It sounds fun, but...
The brain has other plans for us. And it doesn't matter
if you agree, it doesn't matter if you don't know about
them. These plans will always be there, affecting us.

WHAT ARE WE LOOKING FOR?

For fucking around!

And why?!

Because it's cool!

And, how much?!

As much as we can!!

Yay!

Once we learn to connect through the apps, many possible orgasms come into play. How do you want to cum today, baby? Tied to the bed? Sharing it with three more guys? With regulars?

We just go with the flow, having fun, and everything seems to be okay. But while everything seems to be fine, studies reveal how rates of depression and addiction are rising higher and higher, but it's hard to get to the key factor: Why!?

Dopamine appears early on in the equation. Suddenly, we start needing it, and we scroll more and more, and we hose out more and more. Til one day, any hole is good. That's when we might get to the question: What are we really looking for?

The dopamine hit.

- [You] *Wait, but where is the purpose then?*

- [Me] *For Many People... kind of gone.*

THE "SLUT" MACHINE

Like the rest of the book, everything in this chapter is based on research. It's not just *"Daniel saying stuff."* I'm just connecting some dots to make it easier for us to have a conversation as a community. With this being said, get ready, baby.

I want you to imagine the entire process: opening the apps, scrolling and scrolling, finding someone (or not), hosing out or whatever your ritual is, getting to meet, and finally fucking (if they don't ghost you), and compare it to the process in front of a slot machine in Vegas: sitting in front of the machine, putting the money in, hitting buttons, waiting (lights, wheels spinning), and prize (or not).

Any similarities? Uncertainty, waiting periods, relief or not. For the brain, this translates into: cortisol, cortisol, cortisol... boom, dopamine. If things go wrong, since the brain is expecting dopamine, it feels super frustrating, simply because the levels of cortisol are increasing. This will lead to our desperately trying to find the dopamine hit. More apps, more waiting, and finally... aaahhhhh. Dopamine hit.

Frequent exposure to dopamine is addictive. As simple as that. Plus, the contrast between cortisol (stress hormone) and dopamine (high) makes the effects of dopamine create even more pleasant memories in our brain, so we try to find the same feelings we remember.

STAGES OF THE DOPAMINE HUNT

Okay, sweetie. Not everybody is on the dopamine hunt. But it's very easy to fall into it. It all depends on how frequently you expose yourself to dopamine and the "add-ons." Let's separate where our mind could be once we start the dopamine hunt, in three different stages.

Stage 1- If we expose ourselves to this dynamic enough often, we can get addicted.

[This is when we start scrolling "too much"]

Stage 2- If we frequently add extreme sex to the equation, it's even more addictive as it generates higher levels of dopamine.

[This is when we start building "community" with people at the same stage]

Stage 3- If we frequently add drugs (addictive by themselves), the combination is **really** addictive as the dopamine levels skyrocket.

[**This is when we become "regulars" in sex clubs, fisting groups, BDSM groups, and other sex spaces - Weekends are sleepless**]

We could live forever in any of them, but the mechanics of our brain will make us tend to go to Stage 3 and beyond, unless we understand what's happening and take action.

This is the part that I call "The Flaw."

The addictive power of dopamine itself wasn't enough, our brain also had to mess it up!

FROM STAGE 1 TO STAGE 3: THE FLAW

- [Our brain] *Darling, you are giving me so much dopamine that we are going to get addicted! Don't you worry. I have the solution: killing some dopamine receptors of dopamine, so I process less.*

- [Us] *Wait, that means… that the same amount of dopamine will then feel "less?"*

- [Our brain] *That's it.*

- [Us] *We don't want that!*

- [Our brain] *Expose me less to dopamine and I won't have to do that.*

- [Us] *What if we don't?*

- [Our brain] *You will seek more extreme experiences, more drugs and more frequency in order to feel as good as you remember.*

- [Us] *So, once we are in the loop of dopamine hunting... things will only get "worse?"*

- [Our brain] ...

Do you know what the problem is? We can never have that conversation with our brain.

It just happens. And even when we detect signs of danger in our own behavior... dopamine wins.

There we go again.

Once you are in the loop of dopamine hunting, you will always need more and more. You don't need to agree, sweetie. It's what it is. I wish it wasn't this way too!

HOW DOES IT FEEL?

Here is the tricky part. Just like the trauma bond in toxic relationships, gambling or any kind of addiction, it feels like a pull. Like something bringing you naturally back to the same dynamic. In this process, the brain is interpreting chemicals and withdrawal as feelings. Let me break it down:

When we are in the "lows," we feel empty, disconnected, not good enough... but all this is not the real you thinking. This is chemistry cheating your mind. That's when we get the idea to come back on Friday with no regrets. Then we'll experience dopamine. Sex will feel better, connections will feel stronger, and simple things will feel way better than what someone less addicted would experience from the outside. Our perception is not really ours any more. It's distorted. We will remember those experiences and long for them.

This can lead us to a fake sense of connection, to a community not based on healthy habits, and many other things...

Before you scream, it's not me saying it! Research has shown it.

PULLING US BACK

Do you know why sometimes we have a bad day and we end up fucking and the day feels better? At least for a while? It's not fucking, wanking, or cumming itself, sweetie pie. It's dopamine.

We have experienced the contrast of cortisol and dopamine enough times for our brain to learn: *"Dopamine is the solution to this shit."*

So even for people out of the dopamine hunt, the apps will always be a good place to turn to on a bad day, right?

So let's say that sex can become like a bandaid for our pain. The pain of life.

This is how we start getting in and out of Stage 1.

Do we fuck more when we are having a harsh time?

SHARED HIGH = EMOTIONAL INTIMACY

Possibly all your friends are amazing and you have gorgeous connections, so let me talk about Many People.

Many People think they have real friends. They even support each other, but there are so many things they don't like about each other. Maybe they are critical behind each other's back. Different core values, different tastes... But "mysteriously" there they are, one more Friday. Ready to hit the ground til Sunday afternoon. Those are "friends" who support the same dynamic. Connected by the hunt for dopamine.

Before Many People start screaming: Many People, stop doing drugs. Stop participating in certain dynamics at least for a while. You'll see where your friendships go. I think in English it is called "away." And I don't mean distance.

It's also called isolation. When Many People see that the **real** and **healthy** connections they had are eroded by not taking enough care or prioritizing them, and those up for anything "sex-besties" are… still on the hunt. The easiest solution to feel connected again and to stop the fucking withdrawal Many People feel? To come back. No, sweetie. Not back to nurturing those great connections lost along the way. I mean back to the "self-destroying-party" that keeps Many People "connected."

WHY ARE YOU SAYING ALL THIS?

Because our brains confuse **chemical synchrony** with **emotional intimacy**.

When two or more people go through an intense experience at the same time (sex, drugs, danger, dancing for hours, screaming lyrics) their bodies start to **fire together:**

- **Dopamine** floods the reward system. That's the *"this feels amazing, do it again"* signal.

- **Oxytocin** (the bonding hormone) and **endorphins** also rise during sexual touch, laughter, and shared euphoria. They tell the body, I'm safe here. I belong.

- When another person's face, smell, or voice is present while these chemicals peak, your brain **tags them as the source** of safety and pleasure.

- Later, when the high fades, the memory of that person is literally wired together with the memory of the high.

It's our biology doing shortcut math:

same time → same feeling → we're close.

Simple.

That's why people who dance at a rave, survive an accident, trip on the same drug, or orgasm together can feel *soul-bonded* after knowing each other for an hour. The body doesn't distinguish between shared euphoria and deep trust. Both release the same "stuff."

The problem is that the effect is temporary. When dopamine and oxytocin drop, the connection feels weaker, and many of us mistake that chemical withdrawal for rejection or emptiness. So we go back for another shared high, another party, another session, another "Gurl! We vibe so much!" to rebuild what was never emotional in the first place.

That's the trap:

Chemistry masquerading as closeness.

BODY-ODY-ODY

I'm creating the lyric for a new hit song:

"Six-packs,
Eight-day-weeks of gym routines,
steroids to be enough,
Protein shakes
and diets
and diarrhea [diarrhea!]

[Instrumental - hands up, bitches]

[x2]
Hosing out.
Hosing out.
Everybody hosing out.

The bursitis in our shoulder
will never stop us…"

Boom!! Let's get creative, baby. Do you know any producers?

Back to us. Who TF is going to the gym, sweetie pie…? What version of us is getting so obsessed? What version of us is needing to "fit in" so bad? And, how much more do we need?

Let's look at it raw, baby. It's not only that sports is a release… guess what? Dopamine, yes.

It's not that we have sex in the showers… No, sweetie. There is something bigger and we know it.

Problems around self-acceptance? Trying to follow standards? Trying to be good enough for "Stage X?" Social validation? Sex validation?

… Ouch.

What subconsciously is pulling us back into the gym is not the casual sex in the showers.

It's trying to "fit in." It's trying to stay connected. Then, we can love ourselves.

Maybe.

It doesn't matter what stage of the dopamine hunt we're in. Once we are on the hunt, the gym becomes important. Our belly could kick us out of the sex troupe. Out of the apps grid.

- **[Jason]** *Shut up and pass me the steroids. I need to be more liked.*

- **[Me]** *Sure, sweetie. Do you want to try my dealer?*

33

On the way to filling up some emptiness, Many People obsessively transform their bodies to stay on the market. The harness needs to fit perfectly for Folsom…

TALKING ABOUT FOLSOM… WHAT ABOUT BEARS?

Gym obsession and dysmorphia can be two of the side effects of the dopamine hunt. It doesn't mean that's it.

The main problem here is not gym or no gym. It is the frequency of exposure to high levels of dopamine, and how the dopamine hunt can impact our lifestyle and our bodies.

Anyways, it doesn't matter how we label ourselves. I want to throw some things out there to reflect on:

1. Self-Acceptance and Resignation are not the same.

2. "Self-Acceptance" based on dysmorphia… maybe is not self-acceptance.

FROM CONDOMS TO "COND-WHAT??"

I know it's obvious. I know you know about this.

- **[Many People]** *We're lost.*

- **[Us]** *Do we really need to explain to you that sex without protections feels more risky, so it helps with the whole dopamine thing???*

I remember when I was young… and I was so strict with condoms, swallowing or not… Ha!

Then, as I was traveling through the stages of the dopamine hunt, I became more relaxed… kind of careful though.

Then Prep came! It was almost impossible to get it in my first year in Madrid.

I said almost… Wow… just wow…

Then I moved to the US and even though I didn't really need too much (for personal reasons), I got it from my doctor and started saving the bottle, month after month.

Some 2-1-1 here and there...

Til one day, my ears heard "condoms" and my mind went *"cond-what??"*

Does any of this sound familiar, sweetie?

What one day was risky, now doesn't scare many of us. Why?

SAVINGS MODE

The brain hates wasting energy on surprise.

What starts as danger eventually turns into routine if you repeat it often enough.

The first time you cross a line—no condom, higher dose, new stranger—you get a cocktail of dopamine + adrenaline + fear... It's thrilling. Your brain says, *"Wow, survival plus pleasure... let's remember this combo!"* and it records that whole scene as *important*.

Next time you do the same thing, the brain releases a little less adrenaline and a little more dopamine. It's learning that this "danger" didn't kill you. So it moves the experience from the *alarm* folder to the *reward* folder. That's how **desensitization** is born.

Keep repeating it, and what once felt extreme starts to feel *normal*.

- The rush fades.

- The threshold rises.

- The brain craves a stronger spark to feel the same buzz.

So, you up the dose, skip another limit, mix in a bit more risk—because the chemistry of *"oh my god!"* slowly turns into *"meh."*

It's not that we're reckless by nature; it's that the whole dopamine system is "designed" for **novelty and escalation** (do you remember the brain killing dopamine receptors too?)

If the lion doesn't scare you anymore, you will walk closer to it. Maybe one day it will bite.

That's what happens with the dopamine hunt: We chase new intensity to wake the receptors again, forgetting that what's waking them is also numbing them.

So yes, sweetie, what one day was risky no longer scares us.

The brain has quietly re-labeled danger as *familiar pleasure*.

JASON

Poor Jason. He's been a regular in the fisting community of Phoenix a few years. He's a pro.

He recently went to a Beyoncé concert in LA and connected with a guy. Let's just call him Sweetie. They shared some bumps in the portable potties, while kissing and breathing the scents of macro-concerts. They touched… they were horny AF.

Amazing weekend. Unforgettable. Approaching chaos disguised as connection.

- [Us] *Jason, did you tell him about your stuff…?*

- [Jason] *No… But I would be willing to stop extreme sex if I had a relationship with him.*

  [Poor Jason chuckles]

- [Us] *Sure! Why not start a new relationship just hiding it?*

- [Jason] *Yeah.*

[Next weekend - Fresh Jason and Fresh Sweetie - LA weekend date]

Poor Jason has hosed out up to the elbow. He's ready. Not really sure that Sweetie is a top, though.

Waiting for our Sweetie. They go take a walk, see the sunset, eat some pizza with beers… and go to the hotel.

Do you think Jason is going to be ready when his wiener decides to abandon him because just fucking doesn't hit hard enough?

[Jason is freaking out - It simply doesn't work - Sweetie looks at it… the wiener is so dead - Jason is in his head - Poor Jason]

- [Me] *Sweetie, open your kit. Saint Cialis!!*

For a moment Jason's heart feels some relief. Now he just has to answer a few uncomfortable questions like "Are you okay?" and entertain him for 30 minutes talking about his childhood traumas.

Finally, he can perform.

- [Us] *Good job, Jason!*

Jason… so unaware of the brain chemistry running the show. But for you, my flamingo-shaped sweetie pie, long story short:

It didn't work.

Disinterest.

They didn't even need a conversation.
    Simply, two nervous systems wired in different ways.
    Pulling back to their different "natures."
    To their different needs for dopamine…?
    As simple as that. As sad as that. Same core values, interests… all "away."

THE FAKE SENSE OF "I LOVE IT"

Sweetie… let's go inside the control room.

Picture your brain like in the movie *Inside Out*, except some of us have a DJ set instead of the control table and our neurons are shouting over our club music:

*"**Priority:** Keep this bitch alive.*

Secondary: Repeat whatever just felt amazing."

The main procedure here is a sneaky rule called **wanting over liking.**

WANTING VS. LIKING

This means that "I can't stop thinking about it" is not necessarily liking.

Your brain runs two related but different systems:

- **Liking:** actual pleasure/satisfaction in the moment. Warm, complete, "ahhh."

- **Wanting:** drive, pull, obsession, "I need more." That's the attention magnet.

The hunt trains **wanting** to get louder than **liking**. So when your mind says *"I love it/I love him/I love this,"* what it often means is:

"Wanting is screaming so loudly it has borrowed Love's microphone." Something like that.

That's not romance, baby. It's not even liking. That's the brain marking something as *high-priority to pursue,* even if the actual pleasure has been… mid-range. Our brain is not looking for that activity anymore, but for what it causes in it.

THE BRAIN'S "PLOT TWIST!" MACHINE

Your brain is constantly predicting what comes next. When reality **exceeds** expectation…boom, there's a learning spike:

- New face

- New drug

- New body

- New scene

- New you

This *"plot twist!"* creates a stamp in your memory: *"This was special."* The stamp is nothing tender, sweetie, it's technical. The control room adds a star to the cue: that smell, that voice note, that hallway light at 3:12 a.m.

Later, when any of those cues return, the system fires up **wanting** again and our mouth says:

"This is amazing." "I love this." And other "I'm high as fuck" variations.

No, sweetie. Your brain filed a five-star surprise receipt and wants a sequel.

Cue → Craving → Let's make it happen

Here's the loop:

1. A cue shows up (notification ping, a song, a text bubble, that new party, that next orgy...)

2. **Wanting** activates, attention narrows, body leans forward.

3. Mind hates gaps. So it **builds a story** to explain the intensity… and the withdrawal:

   o *"We all have chemistry."*
   o *"We are different."*
   o *"This feels like destiny."*

Intensity arrives first; **meaning** gets painted on top. That painted meaning is the *"I love it"* illusion.

WHY TUESDAY FEELS EMPTY?

(State-dependent attachment)

When you feel something in an altered state, the memory binds to that state. The club, the light, the bass, the scent, your nervous system says:

"These conditions = connection/fun times."

On Tuesday, different lighting, different heartbeat, different you… the signal fades. You don't miss *the party* as much as **you miss the state your body was in.** So the control room whispers:

"Recreate the state, baby."

And we do. And that feels like love, real friendship, great sex, connection… fun! But it's called **state-dependent attachment.**

LIKE WEARING HORSE BLINDS.

(Attentional tunnel)

Under the influence of strong *"wanting,"* the brain narrows vision to the goal. Consequences and alternatives lose color. This is why perfectly good people become simple *background blur* while the most chaotic being can look like a neon soulmate. It's not proof of fate; it's just attentional capture.

THE "EVERYONE ELSE IS BORING" LIE.

(Devaluation of alternatives)

When something or someone is tagged as high-priority, the brain quietly downgrades others. Not because they're worse, but because our filter has changed. The system fucks up our perception to keep the chase efficient. You know.

The control room calls it resource allocation. Efficiency, baby!

THE CAPCUT OF OUR BRAIN

(Memory editing)

Your brain doesn't store every second. It keeps the highlights: the peak, the relief, the wow. Boredom, awkward pauses, *"are you okay?"* moments, edited out. Later you recall a glittery trailer and wonder why we're craving the rerun. Because we saved the best 12 seconds and called it *"I love this."*

THE QUEENS

(Social echo)

Friends cheer the drama, the group chat loops the story, the selfie gets hearts. External signals mirror our internal wanting, amplifying certainty:

"See? Everyone says we're iconic. The Queens."

Maybe. But we are normally algorithmic, not iconic. External echo turns neurochemistry into an identity performance. Now the control room has a new boss: Attention and social validation.

WHERE'S THE MICROPHONE

Now we know… our biology was trying to help us repeat what felt extraordinary. It mislabeled intensity as intimacy, prediction as destiny, wanting as connection.

Real connection might still be here. Quiet, unfashionable, present.

But we'll only hear it when the headset takes
a breath, the intensity fades, and liking gets the
microphone back.
Until then, let's just be kind to our brain.
It wasn't being toxic.
It was being efficient.

IN THE NAME
OF FREEDOM

I remember a guy in San Francisco who called me "stiff" and other adjectives . He was trying to convince me to fuck with him and the rest of the people in the room. He was giving me lessons about sex and freedom. I felt pity. For him, of course. He would only have chem-sex and cocaine and K, even on weekdays. He was talking from addiction. Pushing. Using freedom as a flag, trying to drag me into the same "freedom" that had him trapped.

Addicted people push. Try to convince themselves and others. We always need to keep in mind that NO means NO, in every language, in every community. So, if one day you see yourself pushing, think about this: Who is really talking?

If you are feeling pushed by someone, remember that no social standards or need to satisfy someone else are worth crossing the limits of who you truly are. Protect your boundaries. Also be aware of the presence of abusers in our community, where they thrive in sexual dynamics. Careful, sweetie pie. Sex should happen with consent. Make sure it is respected. If someone calls you stiff, old, boring, while talking about freedom, simply know that probably, it's not their true self talking.

DON'T WASTE TOO MUCH TIME IN CIRCULAR ARGUMENTS, SWEETIE...

In our community, freedom and sexual openness are normally connected. And I agree. But here's the thing: Freedom doesn't keep you trapped in the same dynamic weekend after weekend, year after year.

Addiction does.

Every sexual preference is amazing. But when we get on the dopamine hunt, our own sexual preferences become the channel, not the goal. The channel to finish with the one annoying thing: withdrawal from dopamine.

A WAR CALLED "*OPENNESS*"

Have you ever had an open relationship? Did you end up experiencing some kind of "war" where you were fucking because they did? Don't answer, baby.

"Openness" can be beautiful and freeing. The way to keep it healthy is to stay on the same page. Even if both people are inside the dopamine hunt, but at the same stage, it can work, and it can be amazing.

But now, imagine these scenarios where you and I are a beautiful couple:

You are out of the dopamine hunt. I'm Stage 3. You are Stage 1 or 2. I'm Stage 3.

As you see, you are always the less dopamine affected and I'm high AF.

Do you know what the most frequent result is going to be?

SOMEONE'S BOUNDARIES ARE GOING TO GET PUSHED.

Your boundaries.

You decide what to do with them in order to be loved, or to belong.

When things hurt, we try to find the solution. If they do, you do. Not because you really want to fuck more, but because pain is keeping you stuck in cortisol and your brain needs to find a solution. That's when we rush to open the apps and *"Kpawww!"*

You see "openness" can feed the loop of cortisol-dopamine (among others) and this fucks up our minds.

The same thing happens with sex-buddies. In the name of *"freedom"* and *"openness,"* they'll push. They know how good it feels and they want "the best for you." It's like trying to make you taste the best food in the world because they know it's fucking good.

But, sweetie, who is really pushing? Is it really them? Or is it just a war created by dopamine?

I DO IT, BUT I'M NOT REALLY INTO THAT

Have you ever heard that? Have you ever said it?

In most cases, it's a lie. The truth for Many People would be something like:

"I'm there. I like it.

I also want a Disney love story.

Let's try to have it all."

… Sweetie? How are we doing?

Either you lie or you are lied to… it is not gonna end up okay. We can see ourselves in the middle of a VERY weird story if we detect this behavior and still move on with a relationship where both people are in different stages or directly out of the dopamine hunt.

If this behavior is kind of reasonable because ultimately we are trying to have a genuine relationship while dealing with our dopamine withdrawals, then we lie to protect it.

MISTAKE!

Imagine that we identify that we might be in Stage 3 and trying to connect with a Stage 1 person. Then, the situation should be different. We should be aware of what we are bringing into the relationship and how that's going to impact the life of the other person. Maybe, a little honest dialogue would be great. Kind of:

"Hey, I normally have this type of sex life. It has been like that for years.

Stopping might be difficult.

As my partner, do you accept the challenges I might go through?"

Do you think this would ever happen?

Do you think we will push that new person into our dynamic, because dopamine is more powerful than will?

We can do whatever we want. We can choose our life. But we have to be responsible for others. Just as we don't push people to smoke cigarettes, we shouldn't be pushing people into a **lifestyle** that can trap them. I'm not talking about introducing someone into BDSM. I'm talking again about being responsible with **frequency** and people's boundaries and limits.

HEARTS PUMPING HARD

Should we call it Stage 4? Or simply, the end of the hunt?

Slowly, one by one, we see them falling, like a grotesque version of *"Who's Who."*

First someone you barely knew; you just saw him here and there in the sex clubs.

Then, it's not only one person anymore, and it seems to be getting closer to your loved ones.

One day it happens. It hits too hard. That friend.

His heart just pumped too hard...

Overdosed.

And let's face it. One day, we could lose the game too.

Is it hard, sweetie? It's even harder when our fear and our pain don't stop us. It's as if putting dopamine on a leash was simply out of the discussion. And we keep playing. Forgetting for a while, only to then face the low. And a weird silence that contains our pain. It comes on quickly and nobody wants to break it. But that buddy... is also "away."

ONE MORE TIME, PUERTO VALLARTA!

[You and me preparing for a trip to Puerto Vallarta]

- [Me] *Essential kit for the "up-to-date" gay:*

Imodium

Cialis

Viagra, we get those there

Hosing out device

Bumpies: CC, Holly Molly, K, G, and others.

Stretching tools. If you see one of those orange cones on the highway, put it in the trunk! Yay!

Xanax

And a little bit of Magnesium.

That's all we need, sweetie.

Prepare the Samsonite.

Keep it handy, because we'll repeat it every weekend.

Yay! Freedom! Cool!

My Sniffles is ON, what about yours?

Yassssss, bad bitches that we are.

[Me and you - Waking up in the same room - Destroyed - Plane is leaving - Hurry, bitch]

- **[Me]** *Bumpy to survive?*

- **[You]** *Sure.*

[Me and you in the plane]

- **[Us]**

We did it again, bitch.

Yes…

I think I need to stop this.

Me too.

I'm doing it too often.

Me too.

...

[Four days later - Withdrawal hitting hard]

Sweetie...? Check this out!

A new party awaits. A *"new same weekend."*

- **[You]** *Til when?*

- **[Me]** *Til our bodies resist, baby.*

  Til we decide to stop.

  Til our hearts pump too hard, maybe.

- **[You]** *When did all this happen?*

  When did we really start this hunt?

- **[Me]** *I don't know, my sweetheart.*

  But a long time ago, we were just trying to connect.

THE END

(IS OURS)

WHY, DANIEL...?

Following my purpose of helping queer souls break free from abusive relationships, I learned about the mind. Once I saw, I couldn't unsee. I connected some dots I was wondering about and I started ripping off the bandaids I had put on my own wounds. So I started to face it: My sense of connection was fucked up. Ever since, my choices have been, I don't know if *better* is the word, but way more aware.

I have kept it inside of me for years. The information in this book has come out at a couple events, always timidly. People always screamed back: Freedom!!

I knew that to give this information a chance to shake the room, I needed to expose it in an impactful way. And here we are, sweetie.

I wanted a few things...

... I wanted you to plan your next weekend **KNOWING.**

... I wanted to initiate a conversation, not to finish it.

... I wanted to save us from overdose.

I'm aware that this work is a synthesis. Some technical details about dopamine and related concepts are intentionally left out. Getting more precise would've taken this piece into a different format.

The world needs awareness more than perfection. If you know more, please share it with love.

Rage won't take us anywhere near happiness.

If this brief work made you reflect in a different way, please share it with others. My goal was to create a very digestible but impactful conversation starter. If you think it worked, your honest review would mean a lot to me.

Thank you for sharing this time with me.

Daniel.

Sweetie, you deserve care. If you think stopping is not enough, or you find it difficult, please, make that call.

RESOURCES

USA

- 988 Suicide & Crisis Lifeline — Call/Text 988 (24/7). https://988lifeline.org. Spanish available.

- SAMHSA National Helpline (mental health & substance use info/referrals) — 1-800-662-HELP (4357). www.usa.gov/agencies/substance-abuse-and-mental-health-services-administration

- The Trevor Project (LGBTQ youth 24/7) — 1-866-488-7386, chat/text via site. www.thetrevorproject.org

- Trans Lifeline (peer support by trans operators) — US 877-565-8860. www.translifeline.org

- Gay & Sober (LGBTQ recovery meetings/resources) — Directory & support online. www.gayandsober.org

- National Harm Reduction Coalition (overdose prevention, syringe access info; not a hotline) — resources online. https://harmreduction.org

UK

- NHS Urgent Mental Health Help — Call 111 and select the mental health option (24/7, nationwide). www.bsmhft.nhs.uk/service-users-and-carers/how-to-get-urgent-mental-health-help

- Samaritans (24/7 listening support) — 116 123. www.samaritans.org/how-we-can-help

- Switchboard: National LGBTQIA+ Helpline — 0300 330 0630, email/chat via site. https://switchboard.lgbt

- London Friend – Antidote (LGBTQ drug/alcohol & chemsex support) — 020 7833 1674, antidote@ londonfriend.org.uk. https://londonfriend.org.uk

- Talk to FRANK (confidential drug info/advice) — 0300 123 6600, text 82111. https://talktofrank.com

- Mind Helplines guide (SANEline, CALM, Shout, PAPYRUS) — numbers & hours listed. www.mind.org.uk/information-support/guides-to-support-and-services

CANADA

- 9-8-8 Suicide Crisis Helpline — Call/Text 9-8-8 (24/7).
  https://988.ca

- Canada Health – Mental Health Support (federal portal
  with provincial lines).
  www.canada.ca/en/public-health/services/mental-health-
  services.html

- Get help with substance use (federal portal + provincial
  helplines).
  www.canada.ca/en/health-canada/services/substance-use/
  get-help-with-substance-use.html

- Trans Lifeline (Canada) — 877-330-6366.
  https://translifeline.org/hotline/

- Rainbow Health Ontario (2SLGBTQ+ health services
  directory) — info & referrals.
  www.rainbowhealthontario.ca

- CATIE (national HIV/hep C info; chemsex resources) —
  service directory & guides.
  www.catie.ca/resource/sexualized-drug-use-chemsex-and-
  methamphetamine-among-men-who-have-sex-with-men?

AUSTRALIA

- Lifeline — 13 11 14 (24/7 phone), text/chat info on site. www.lifeline.org.au

- Beyond Blue — 1300 22 4636 (phone & webchat). www.beyondblue.org.au

- QLife (national LGBTIQ+ peer support) — 1800 184 527, webchat (3pm–midnight daily). https://qlife.org.au

- ACON – Alcohol & Other Drugs / Chemsex (M3THOD) — counselling + peer programs. www.acon.org.au/what-we-are-here-for/alcohol-drugs

Do you feel trapped in your relationship?

Visit www.thesparkletrap.com

The Sparkle Trap: Recognizing, "Escaping," and Healing from Narcissistic Abuse in LGBTQ+ Love

I'm Daniel de Llano!

Don't hate me too much on social media!

Love is always welcome!

TikTok: @dellano.daniel

Youtube: @thesparkletrap

Instagram: @dellanodani

FURTHER READING / REFERENCES

This brief list brings together works that explore queer identity, intimacy, trauma, pleasure, dopamine, addiction, and the psychology of connection. These texts informed my own healing journey and expanded the lens through which I wrote *Interconnected*.

QUEER STUDIES & INTIMACY

- Ahmed, Sara. *Queer Phenomenology: Orientations, Objects, Others*. Duke University Press, 2006.

- Berlant, Lauren, and Michael Warner. "Sex in Public." *Critical Inquiry*, vol. 24, no. 2, 1998.

- Greenwell, Garth. *Cleanness*. Farrar, Straus and Giroux, 2020.

- Preciado, Paul B. *Countersexual Manifesto*. Columbia University Press, 2018.

TRAUMA, ABUSE & EMOTIONAL PSYCHOLOGY

- van der Kolk, Bessel. *The Body Keeps the Score: Brain, Mind, and Body in the Healing of Trauma.* Viking, 2014.

- Herman, Judith. *Trauma and Recovery.* Basic Books, 1992.

- Maté, Gabor. *In the Realm of Hungry Ghosts: Close Encounters with Addiction.* North Atlantic Books, 2010.

DOPAMINE, BEHAVIOR & THE NEUROSCIENCE OF DESIRE

- Anna Lembke. *Dopamine Nation: Finding Balance in the Age of Indulgence.* Dutton, 2021.

- Huberman, Andrew. "The Biology of Desire, Craving, and Pleasure." *The Huberman Lab Podcast,* 2021–2023.

- Schultz, Wolfram. "Dopamine Reward Prediction Error Coding." *Neuron,* vol. 80, no. 2, 2013.

CHEMSEX, COMMUNITY & SEXUAL CULTURE

- Race, Kane. *Pleasure Consuming Medicine: The Queer Politics of Drugs.* Duke University Press, 2009.

- Stuart, Jake. *Chemsex: Drugs, Pleasure, and Sexuality.* Zed Books, 2020.

- Bourne, Adam et al. "The Chemsex Study." *London School of Hygiene & Tropical Medicine,* 2014.

CONNECTION, LONELINESS & EMOTIONAL HEALING

- Hari, Johann. *Lost Connections*. Bloomsbury, 2018.

- Brown, Brené. *Daring Greatly*. Avery, 2012.

- Cozolino, Louis. *The Neuroscience of Human Relationships*. Norton, 2006.

This list is not meant to be exhaustive; it reflects the constellation of ideas, research, and personal inquiries that shaped my understanding of desire, connection, and the ways queer bodies seek meaning in a world that often misunderstands us.

CREDENTIALS

- Member of the International Association of Counselors and Therapists (IACT - USA)

- Accredited with the Association of Counsellors, Coaches, Psychotherapists and Hypnotherapists (ACCPH - UK)

- Certified Hypnotherapist specializing in RTT (Rapid Transformational Therapy)

- Mindvalley Certified Coach

- Royal Higher College of Performing Arts (Madrid, Spain)

I'm all that, and I research the mind. But I'm *not* a therapist, and this work is *not* a substitute for professional advice.